Sensual Romance Titles by Mercedes
Bleau

Books of the Magkean

WOLF CLAIMED
WITCH BETRAYED (Coming 2016)

Kingdom of Nareth

FARBO
LUSTEN (Coming 2016)

Farbo

A story of the Kingdom of Nareth

By Mercedes Bleau

Alpha Witch Publishing
2885 Sanford Ave SW #33978
Grandville, MI 49418

alphawitch.com

FARBO

Look for other titles by Mercedes Bleau at
www.mercedesbleau.com
This is a work of fiction. Names, characters, places, and incidents
either are the product of the author's imagination or are used
fictitiously, and any resemblance to actual persons, living or dead,
business establishments, events, or locales is entirely coincidental.

For information address: Alpha Witch Publishing
2885 Sanford Ave SW #33978, Grandville, MI 49418
info@alphawitch.com.

Book ISBN: 978-0-692-57542-0
Publishing History
Alpha Witch eBook edition January 2016

Cover Design by M.M.

Glossary of Terms

Blood Den: Noble sanctioned feeding house for unmated Todesgeist.

Blood Mother: The appointed head of a Blood Dén. This is a lifelong appointment. An honorable title for those of the Kuspit. They are the keepers of race.

Demimorden: Un-blooded humans. Short lived lesser cousins of the Todesgeist.

Denkin: Inhabitants of the Blood Dén, who report to the Appointed Blood Mother.

Farbo: Second part of the Todesgeist Satiation. The food of the soul. The very energy of life and creation. This energy is released only during full satiation during which all three seats of power are opened in complete supplication. Often only released after a full feeding of both Lusten and San during the height of climax. The culminating point of the Satiation Ritual.

Kuspit Noble: High nobles born of lineage descendant of the original six. Traceable family books magically bound, and spelled against untruths are kept at every family seat.

Lusten: First part of the Todesgeist Satiation. The food of the body. The very essence of physical need and sustenance. Energy released by the body during physical arousal and pleasure.

MorderBan: Mid Class Blood Den located in Southern California. See Lusten.

RedMorder: High class Blood Den located in Nevada. See Blood Mother.

Reticine: Trusted Protector. More closely defined as Keeper. As Todesgeist require the full satiation in order to survive upon coming of age, it is customary for females of the Noble Kuspit to be appointed a keeper. This is to keep the coveted females safe, but also to prevent them from having to scavenge to survive. The Reticine is responsible for meeting his mistress's every need.

San: Third part of the Todesgeist Satiation. The food of the heart. Energy garnered through drinking the blood of others.

Sangeisten: Literally Noble Protectors. Noble sect of the original six families that have formed into separate military police group, responsible for the longevity, security, and protection of the secret of the race's existence.

Satiation: Todesgeist feeding ritual whereby all three hungers are fed. Lusten, Farbo, San. Known as a full feeding. Upon coming of age the séne is broken by initiating a full feeding, during which the soul weile, or Farbo seat is opened for the first time. This releases the powers of the soul and reveals the Farbo marks that declare a Todesgeist's status in the Kingdom.

Séne: Uninitiated. A Todesgeist who has never experienced a full satiation is said to be this.

Tellrian Band: Lesser nobles fallen or unclaimed by a greater family but belonging to a lesser family.

Todesgeist: Members of the Kingdom of Nareth. Vampires like you've never seen before. Long lived, strong, powerful, and Oh so Hawt!!

Wéile: The door to the inner power of all Todesgeist. The heart and soul of the being and the essence of life.

Zabine Denizen: Unaffiliated Todesgeist with untraceable origins, or lineage to the Original six. Are often mercenaries, work for hire, artists, artisans, etc. They are few as here are many benefits to being affiliated. Most children are adopted, or join other families.

CONTENTS

Lusten, Farbo, San, the three parts of the Todesgeist satiation. We are vampire, or rather those of the Kingdom of Nareth. The Sire, the original Todesgeist fell to the earth and created from his blood and seed six children. He bid them spread with the Demimorden, the humans of all realms, to dilute the blood so that we might find harmony and peace. The six chose six mates from six of the seven realms leaving the seventh realm of death untouched. They were left to breed for many years until they were called upon by the Sire. There he began the Ritual.

This is our legend. We are many. We are Kuspit Nobles, Tellrian Band, Sangeisten, and Zabine Denizens. These are the four orders of the Kingdom of Nareth. We are not free to live, but it is true that ritual serves more than chaos ever could. The ritual is existence, our legend in live evolution. It is for us and those we would share this world with. Without it we are lost.

-Portia Liebemorder, Blood Mother

CHAPTER ONE

Her body bowed bending upward, chest curving backward in a dancer's arc, even as her hips worked in frenzied abandon. She thrust herself into the lapping tongue, her arms stretching along the soft silk of sweaty sheets. *Lusten* was heavy in the air, blanketing the room in its cool life giving essence.

It was always this way when the Mistress was served by her Reticine. Him worshiping her with his mouth and body, wringing cries of overwrought pleasure from pursed lips, and sweat from a perfectly formed brow. He, her Sayber, was always silent and strong, his motions firm and practiced.

Atlyn wanted to turn away from the scene in front of her, her eyes watered with the need, but she couldn't. She'd been strapped to the chair again. Punished for some imagined wrong. Made to watch as her Mistress engaged in the Ritual and she was denied.

The silver strap that wreathed her forehead

prevented her from turning her head. The bracelets at her wrists and shackles at her ankles prevented her from moving even an inch from her seat behind the billowing blue curtains. For two days and two nights she had been forced to sit in this chair.

Holding in a deep sigh Atlyn let her eyes lose focus, the writhing bodies before her becoming blurred forms through a window covered in ice. The *Lusten* beckoned but she was not allowed to take in its candied essence. She had been banned from the *Ritual* yet again.

She felt her heart stutter at the sharp flavor of *San* that seemed to suddenly be everywhere at once. Blinking she saw that her Mistress had sank her fangs into Sayber's neck just at the curve of his shoulder.

Blinking back tears she gripped her hands into fists, ignoring the pain of her short nails biting through the skin of her palm. Sayber was *hers*. Atlyn forced the thought from her mind refusing to let it take root.

If her Mistress ever found out what he was to Atlyn, it would be one more weapon in her closet of tortures. She would make Atlyn suffer at every opportunity. Such was the nature of the woman she was bound to. For now.

She'd thought it was fortunate to be fostered to the Great Myca MorderBan. A Ritual blessing to be apprenticed to one such as her. Atlyn's mother had been a dancer of the highest order, revered in all circles of the Noble Kuspit. That had been before she'd known what that would actually mean. There could never be another as great as Myca, and she made sure that her lowly apprentice would never forget that.

One pink tear escaped from Atlyn's eye winding quickly over her cheek to curve softly around the edge of her mouth. The only brightness in her life was Sayber. Her destined mate, here with her, so close she could feel the heat from his body. Her Mistress gasped as she was entered forcefully from below, Sayber gripping her hips as he worked himself in and out of her wet channel.

Atlyn new she must not close her eyes; she had been punished for that before. Her certainty was confirmed a few moments later as she felt her mistress's gaze fall on her from the bed. They taunted her like small daggers making stinging cuts along her body. Atlyn forced her face to remain impassive, gripped her fists so hard they ached.

As if sensing her gleeful focus Sayber turned his mistress to her stomach, and fisting the hard shaft at the root guided himself into her ready channel again. His mouth took hers in a punishing kiss as his hands slid beneath her pelvis to fondle the erect nubbin that bloomed from silky moist skin.

"Who do you punish this night Mistress?"

His voice was gravel deep and dark with sensual promise. Atlyn barely held in a moan at the sound of it. Simply listening to him talk was an unparalleled delight. Her mate.

"The same one as always."

His hips paused a moment, and he covered the fault by lifting Myca's bottom high in the air as he pressed her chest into the mattress. He began to lunge inside her, the sound of wet skin meeting wet skin punctuating each harsh thrust. Myca's moan was guttural and she shivered beneath him, throwing her hips into each profound stroke.

Eyes the color of a midnight sea searched the semi-shear curtain that covered the small corner of the room. Atlyn watched as the muscles in his square jaw tensed as if he were grinding his teeth. Then his eyes found hers through the darkness that shrouded her. Did he know? The moment was gone just as quickly as it came, the connection broken as Sayber slid his fangs into the skin at Myca's back.

A short scream then the shuttering breath of orgasm followed by the quick wispy rush of *Farbo* completed their satiation. Their bodies clung together, wet with sweat, as Sayber pulled his still erect cock from his mistress's well saturated body. He sat on the edge of the bed, one square hand running through the short black hair on his head.

He looked tired. His Farbo markings were an intricate line across his chest and ringing his upper arms. The elaborate golden symbols declared his status as a member of the Noble Kuspit more clearly than anything else. Every initiated Todesgeist revealed order markings after coming of age. It was one more thing that her mistress had denied her.

Atlyn could see the lines of strain at the edges of his mouth, the weariness that seemed to cloud his vision sometimes when he thought no one was looking. She wanted to stroke a gentle hand over that troubled brow, to lay light kisses up the strong jaw. She ached with it. Instead she remained a prisoner in the chair, forced to witness as another took what was destined to be hers.

"Your patron is here Mistress, waiting in the lower salon for you to appear." Sayber reminded. He stood, moving to the basin against the far wall to wash.

"I know." Myca smiled moving languidly as she slid from the bed stretching long slim limbs before her. "I needed to feed before tonight's performance, Tand always demands that I be in perfect form for him."

Slipping the floor length robe over her firm body Myca let the front gape open, revealing well-loved nipples still pink and erect from Sayber's attention. Her hair was a pale curtain over her shoulders and down to the middle of her back.

"You can let that one go, I think she's learned her lesson," She said almost as an afterthought as she floated from the room.

Dark eyes found hers again and Atlyn gasped as her body readied itself, feminine muscles shifting in anticipation as her channel grew immediately damp with womanly cream. It was always thus when she was near her mate, her body's natural reaction to the one destined for it. She was caught by the movement of his hand as it stroked the water from his skin.

"Must you provoke her?" His voice startled her from her trance. He stood facing her now, his erection bobbing in the air as it jutted from his body. She was caught by it, the desire to taste the wetness that had formed at the tip almost overwhelming her.

"My breathing provokes her Sir Reticine. Would you have me stop?"

She'd used his formal title as instructed even though she thought of him as Sayber in her mind. She'd learned that lesson in this very same chair not two weeks after she'd come of age.

A quick movement of his arm and the curtains were cast aside revealing her to him. Her nipples puckered against the rush of cool air, and she wished for the hundredth time that she wasn't naked and strapped to a metal chair. Embarrassment was a hot rush in her cheeks but she forced herself to hold his gaze.

His eyes examined her as if he were taking in every minute detail. Their touch was tangible as they ran over her face and down the gentle curves of her body lingering on her swollen breasts and the short cropped hair at the juncture of her thighs.

"Shall I release you?" he asked.

She was struck mute by the promise in his eyes, the sudden interest that shined through for a moment and just as quickly disappeared. He'd never looked at her this way before, never acknowledged her past what was absolutely necessary. What had changed?

"If it pleases you." Another trained response. She was an apprentice, the only needs she was allowed were those she was instructed to have.

"And if it doesn't?"

Atlyn didn't have an answer but was rewarded with a quick flash of perfect white teeth before his flawlessly formed lips moved back into a stern line.

He stepped closer bringing the scalding head of his aroused flesh just inches from her cheek. She forced herself not to look there, praying that the longing in her body wasn't mirrored in her expression.

"Look at me." His voice had suddenly gone soft, gentle against the ferocity of his arousal. Atlyn forced her eyes to his.

"What will you give me if I release you?"

Her body jerked at his words. They had been ripe with suggestion, the tone a wet tongue sliding between oversensitive breasts. She had never heard him use this tone before. Did he know her? Shaking her head to clear the thought she again focused on the straining cock before her, licking suddenly dry lips.

"Anything."

"How long has it been since you were satiated?"

Never. She'd come of age here in her mistress's home, and had been denied the breaking of her sène. She was allowed to siphon Lusten from the air and to drink blood from willing donors only.

"I took blood from Lydia just five days ago." She whispered.

His eyes widened as if in shock and he frowned for a moment bringing a gentle hand to her cheek. His fingers traced the path her tears had made there, and then he groaned and let his tongue follow them, tasting the salty flavor of her misery.

Atlyn held herself still unable to believe that she was finally feeling the wet rasp of her Sayber's tongue against her skin. She forced herself not to lean into him, but couldn't hold in a small sound at the sudden pain of her hands gripping into fists once more.

Warm hands covered hers forcing her to release the tension she held there. The sound of metal sliding against metal signaled the release of her wrists from their bonds. He kissed each palm as he freed it, gently laving the injuries her nails had made, and ending with a soft press of warm lips right in the center.

Releasing her palm he laid it gently on her thigh then stood again, brandishing that magnificent erection like a sword. It slid against her cheek the silky hardness a burning caress against the skin there.

"What will you give me if I release you?"

She stared at the taught muscles of his abdomen, curling her fingers around each other to keep from reaching out, and rubbing against the smooth tan skin just above his cock. Words clogged her throat, and she swallowed, turning her face slightly into the straining erection, and laying soft lips against the shaft.

"Whatever pleases you Sir Reticine."

His hand gripped her hair wrapping it around his knuckles to anchor her head at the nape. Tilting her head back as far as the metal head band would allow, he looked down into her face, his blue eyes as dark as a windswept shore in the middle of the night. Atlyn waited barely daring to draw a complete breath, hoping that he would take what she had to offer.

He was a trusted protector, an appointed keeper of a female of the Noble Kuspit, but he was free to choose his own company. He would serve Myca until she found her destined mate, and released him from his appointment.

Atlyn still wanted him, even having witnessed him riding her mistress's body just moments before. She craved him, his smell, his touch, his voice was a balm to her ravaged existence, the only brightness in the misery that was forced on her by a cruel master. She would have gladly taken him into her mouth immediately after he'd freed himself from Myca's dripping channel.

"Open your mouth."

FARBO

CHAPTER TWO

She complied, releasing a shallow breath her eyes finding his.

He cupped himself, and then gripped the shaft, guiding the tip to hover just over her tongue.

"Will you take me in your mouth little apprentice?"

Atlyn could only look at him, fighting the urge to beg, or to take what she most desired. He smelled of masculine spice enticing and cinnamon.

"Suck me."

Moaning in absolute supplication, Atlyn took him in her mouth, letting her tongue slide over the tip before sucking him deep inside. Sayber groaned his knees bending slightly as he braced his palm on the chair back behind her head. There was a low metallic click and then her head was freed from the metal strap.

Sayber pushed deep into the soft heat of her, savoring the feeling of her tongue caressing the sensitive area beneath the head. He felt himself tighten, the sudden pleasure of her mouth almost overwhelming him. His hand found the soft curls in her hair, sliding through the shiny red brown locks as she tasted him, seeming to savor the flavor.

She was lovely in her passion, eager and accommodating in a way he hadn't expected. He knew she thought that he ignored her, but nothing could be farther from the truth. Growling low and steady he gently removed himself from the suctioning heat of her mouth, and bent to release her ankles from the shackles that bound her to the chair. She was his. He had suspected for some time now, but with her reaction to him, and his unabating erection whenever he was in her presence he couldn't doubt it any longer.

Lifting her gently into his arms he carried her away from the punishment chair and through an adjoining door to his chambers. His cock ached with the need to slide inside the tight unused channel between her legs. He needed her in a way he'd never imagined. As if he was destined to possess her. She looked up at him her doe eyes gentle and trusting, simply allowing him to do whatever he chose.

"You are forbidden. Did you know?"

"Yes. I am sène at the Mistress's request, though I am well past the age of adulthood."

Her voice was soft, the timbre slightly lower than one would expect by looking at her. She was slender, and small, her waist tiny next to his large form.

You are mine, did you know that?

He wanted to ask her, but paused with the words

on his tongue. Maybe it was better if she didn't know. If the Mistress ever found out he would never be released from his appointment. Myca'd stop at nothing to make this one suffer. Sayber had witnessed the enmity between Myca and Atlyn's mother, though he was sure she knew nothing of the origins of her mistreatment.

He laid her gently on the bed and turned to set the lock on the adjoining door. She sat exactly where he'd left her, her eyes trailing around the room as if in wonder.

"How long were you in the chair?"

"Two days Sir Reticine."

"Sayber. Please at least when we are alone, call me Sayber." Her smile was a gift, if a fleeting one, transforming her elegant face, to shinning beauty. He couldn't resist, leaning down, slowly he rested his lips on hers. She tasted sweet and sexy and suddenly he was moaning into her mouth and pulling her against him. Their tongues caressed each other, and his hands found the rounded curve of her bottom.

"I need you."

She whimpered in response, their ardor renewed at his words. Forcing himself to resist the temptation of her mouth he focused on doing what came as second nature. He could not have his mate, but he would care for her in any way he was able.

Lifting her slight weight he carried her into the bathroom and sat her on the tiled counter. Steeling another quick kiss he turned on the shower and waited for the water to get warm.

"Are you sore?"

She nodded fatigue suddenly visible in her eyes.

"Will you let me take care of you?"

"Yes…Sayber."

His name on her lips was a warm embrace. He smiled, sudden contentment in her presence bubbling to the surface only to subside again. That happened often when he was near her. Yet another sign that she was destined for him. He lifted her into the warm spray and followed behind her sliding the glass door closed.

Her skin was warm and smooth beneath his fingers as he soaped her supple body. She was unblemished and soft, the lack of Farbo markings a declaration of her uninitiated state. They would appear as soon as she opened her *weile* and fed in the full Satiation of their kind. This was only accomplished by feeding all three parts at once. His mate had been forbidden to do this.

His heart hurt at the thought of the treatment that Atlyn had received. Much of it he had been unaware of, but recently he'd noticed the little indignities she'd been made to suffer.

He felt her nipple pucker beneath the pass of his palm, and bent his head to her breast. Suckling the sensitive tip, he slid his tongue over the yielding brown areola before taking her deep into his mouth. His hands continued to smooth soap over her body, the clean citrusy scent mixing with her natural musk as he explored her curves and secret places. He spanned her waist, and then traced down her flat stomach to cup the wet heat of her pussy. She was ready for him, as he'd expected, the gentle folds weeping her arousal onto slender thighs.

Her body vibrated against him, as he shifted to the other nipple leaving the former swollen and well loved. His fingers delved between her nether lips spreading the essence of her womanhood over the delicate skin there. Sliding one finger inside, he stood slowly to capture her moans in his mouth.

Lusten was a glistening sheen in the air, surrounding them in its essence, he felt his fangs extend and let them softly score the sensitive skin on the underside of her breast.

"Yes. Take me Sayber."

The yearning for her blood mixed with his need to possess her body, enhanced the almost painful desire to push the head of his weeping cock into the burning slickness of her cove. He let his fangs slide into the skin around her nipple just breaching the outer layer, and she gripped his hair in her hands her hips pressing into his stomach. Pulling out he cupped her cheeks in his palms and tasted her lips, slowly, gently, before sucking her tongue into his mouth.

The fingers on one hand found the engorged button at the top of her mound as the other gripped the firm flesh of her ass. Her body was a sexual fantasy against him, demanding his attention even as it brought his need to torturous levels. His shaft was pulsing with the craving to taste her channel.

"Take me in your hand baby." His voice was ragged.

She did as he asked sliding her small fist over the head of him to the base.

"Harder. Like this."

His hand covered hers guiding her movements. Sayber vibrated against her fighting the need to pump his hips, denying the instant desire to fuck her fist until he spilled his seed all over her stomach.

Leaning back he pressed her face into his neck.

"Feed from me Li'ya. Take me into you."

It felt like forever before he felt her fangs rasp against the skin of his neck.

"Yes! Take me."

She struck, her soft lips pushing against him and he cried out his hands gripping the curve of her hips, as he helplessly thrust into the tight clasp of her fingers. There was nothing like the pleasure of the bite. He felt her draw on him and it was all he could do not to fall to his knees. She made soft sounds in the back of her throat, and he felt her draw on the *Lusten* in the air as she took the *San* from his blood, feeding the two parts in tandem.

It didn't last long enough, too soon she was licking the small wounds she had made and he was drowning in her kiss, loath to give up the haven of her mouth. His hand replaced hers and he gripped her against him, as he worked the shaft with a firm grip, stopping only to caress the swollen head. Atlyn writhed before him her body slick with water and soap, her hands running over his muscled form as if she wanted to touch all of him at once.

He came hard, the intense spasms of orgasm forcing his seed to gush from the tip of his erection, bathing her stomach in its scalding heat. Before he had finished he fell to his knees his arms wrapping around her round hips, as his tongue delved into the slippery warmth of her. She tasted musky and sensual on his tongue, and he wanted to bury his face against her. Her hands found their way to his head and she gripped him there.

Sayber licked the length of her vulva, then kissing her nether lips he suckled at her opening, firmly tonguing her slit. Alternating between sucking kisses and stimulating penetration he worked himself against her sliding his hands over the crease of her back side and up to cup her soft breasts. She made a noise much like a scream, as he pushed into her pussy tasting the heady essence of her arousal.

Pressing the back of her neck with one hand he brought her mouth to his for a searing kiss and then resumed his sensual torture. Sayber guided her leg over his shoulder as his eyes locked with hers, his breath a hot stimulation against the swollen tissue of her sex.

Her clitoris was engorged, peaking out from the tiny hood as if begging to be sucked. Who was he to resist such an invitation?

He took the small shaft into his mouth drawing gently as his fingers found purchase in the well lubricated cleft of her heat. Penetrating her slowly with two fingers he made love to her with his mouth. His rhythm was steady guided by intermittent lapping of lips and tongue. Atlyn's knees gave way and he held her bottom in his palm cupping the sweetness of her female folds to his mouth. She was frenzied, her hips grinding against him as her hands clutched his head between her thighs.

Her voice was a sharp echo against the gentle roar of the shower as she came, delicate muscles squeezing his fingers as her clitoris throbbed against his tongue. Sayber had never tasted anything sweeter than her pleasure against his lips. He would have been happy to stay where he was for the rest of his life. Even now his cock was bobbing against his stomach in fervent entreaty.

Pushing his own needs aside he cradled the limp body in his arms and carried his would be mate to his bed. She lay boneless on the soft sheets her eyes closing immediately as she fell into a deep sleep. Running the back of his hand over her soft cheek, Sayber covered her with the heavy blanket and turned to dress. She would be safe here for the night, and they'd face whatever tomorrow brought together.

CHAPTER THREE

Warmth and spice. No other male smelled so good. She was in Sayber's bed. Atlyn didn't resist the urge to curl around the knowledge. She wrapped herself in him, wanting only to stay here in his room for the rest of the day. The Mistress would never allow it. If she knew where Atlyn had slept there would be no more quiet moments for anyone.

Sighing gently Atlyn sat up, enjoying the feeling of the soft sheets sliding against her sensitive breasts. She shivered in memory the ghost of Sayber's tongue reminding her of the pleasure that he'd given her. She was brimming with energy like she hadn't felt in years. Sliding her feet to the floor she stood and stretched, reaching slender arms to the ceiling then back arching she let them slowly lower to the wall behind her.

She straitened slowly rolling hips that suddenly felt female and ripe. She'd never known desire such as what she felt for Sayber. Never experienced anything like it. She felt like she'd been asleep her entire life and had just suddenly woken up.

Her room was on the floor below at the end of the other wing of the house. She didn't have any clothes to put on. Looking around her she looked for something to cover her body. She couldn't use any of Sayber's cloths. They were too noticeable. Anyone who saw her would know she'd slept with a male. In any other house, with any other mistress, that would be something to celebrate.

In this house, it was something to hide.

She took a few steps and bending at the waist wrapped her arms around her legs, gripping her ankles. Of course that is exactly the positon she was in when the door opened behind her. She heard a short intake of breath, then was blanketed by a gentle wave of *Lusten* that came from the doorway.

"Are you trying to drive me crazy or is that how you greet all of your visitors."

She laughed, but before she could straiten Sayber was there pressing his hips against the soft skin of her butt. His hands gripped her at the hip pressing her into the erection that tented his loose trousers.

"I didn't expect you to come back so soon." Her voice had a husky quality that she'd never voiced before. She groaned pushing herself back against the solid muscle of the male against her.

"I went to get this." He dropped a garment over her shoulder, making sure the silky coolness of it slid against her skin as it fell.

"Thank you Sir Reticine. May I stand?"

He hesitated, sliding large square hands over the firm cheeks of her backside then around to grip her slender thighs.

"I don't know. I like you just like this. Never thought I'd love the sight of a female's naked pussy pointing right at me as much as I loved yours. Are you trying to torture me? Or was that an invitation?"

Atlyn loved the rough timbre of his voice. It caressed her adding to the fantasy like quality of the moment. She immersed herself in it. Felt the ridged heat of him pressing against the moist entrance to her body. What would it feel like if he pressed himself inside her? Would she feel the slightly flared tip as it stretched her insides? Would the thick slide of him pleasure her as deeply as the mere thought of it did? She shuddered barely managing to stay on her feet.

The words tumbled past her lips. "My body is yours."

Sayber stiffened, then the heat of him was gone. Atlyn wanted to weep with unrequited desire. Why had she said that? She knew that he couldn't claim her. The Mistress would never allow it. She was to remain sène . A punishment for the sin of having been complimented by the Mistress's favorite patron. The only dancer that could receive compliments was Myca. Another unspoken rule of the house.

"I'm sorry." She mumbled gripping the training

robe and covering herself as she straitened. She couldn't quite meet his eyes. His fingers found her chin and applied a gentle pressure until she was forced to look at him.

"You have nothing to be sorry for." Sayber's fingers traced her cheek a moment and then he stepped back, taking his spicy scent with him. "You better go. You have about thirty minutes before you have to be at the bar."

Atlyn nodded, still shaken by the naked desire in his eyes. She felt the bonds of intimacy settle between them, and her heart lifted at the feeling. He wanted her? He knew who she was? She wouldn't ruin it again by speaking of it. She pulled the robe closed, covering her nudity, but she felt more naked now than she'd ever been.

"Tell me something apprentice. Why did you choose to come here? There are several other houses in the Kingdom that you could have trained in."

"This is the best one."

He nodded turning and walking to the bed to sit. "But why did you stay?"

She raised her eyebrows at him.

"Shone told me what it's been like for you. The Mistress hates you. She'll never let you advance to dancer."

Shone was her only friend in the house. He was one of the few males who'd decided to stay after completing his training. He danced with the Mistress when she needed a partner.

"Where could I go? My father died last year. Without a keeper of my own I wouldn't be allowed to live alone in my family house."

Females of the Noble Kuspit were highly valued. She wanted to snort at the very thought. If she had been born Tellrian Band, or Zabine Denizen she could have walked away long ago. No one cared if they lived on their own with no protection.

She had to stay here, or she'd be forced to live in the cloister with the other unclaimed females. Once you went there, it wasn't likely you would ever leave. No males were allowed to enter. How could a female be claimed if she never met any males?

"Why didn't your father find you a keeper?"

"He wanted to. I refused. I was so sure that I'd have all the time I needed. I never thought he'd die the way he did." Atlyn closed her eyes briefly against the sudden pain of loss.

"I'm sorry li'ya."

Her eyes held his a moment. There was another reason she'd never tried to leave. She couldn't bear the thought of being away from him. She would endure any humiliation, any pain to stay here with Sayber. Shaking herself she moved towards the door. It would be better if she didn't voice that last bit.

"Thank you Sir Reticine."

Atlyn let the door close gently behind her and moved quickly down the hall. She felt giddy with emotions that she'd never thought to experience. She was still simmering on the low thrill of arousal that coursed through her.

Picking up her pace she hurried down the stairs and just slipped into the dressing room before the door closed. If she wasn't in her positon before the bar before the Mistress entered the room... Well she'd probably be put back into the chair again. To go back so soon after being set free would be double the torture.

She'd already gone several days without rest and if it hadn't been for Sayber she'd be barely able to stand. He'd taken such good care of her. Massaging her aching muscles and urging her to feed from him again as they'd lain in his soft big bed. Atlyn held in the sigh that threatened to spill from her lips.

Slipping her shoes on she trotted into the dance room and took her place. There were five other apprentices at the bar. Four female and one male. All kept their posture erect and looked straight ahead as they had been trained. Atlyn assumed the same pose and waited for Myca to arrive.

The main door opened and the Mistress stepped into the room. She was dressed as usual in a loose fitting sheer training tunic and leggings. Her feet were bare, and her summery hair pulled into a tight bun at the base of her skull. Her nipples were clearly visible through the shirt, and they were swollen and pink as if they'd just been popped from a hungry mouth.

Myca looked over her students a moment and raised her hand to signal them to begin. She stopped just before giving the go ahead her eyes zeroing in on Atlyn.

"Atlyn!" her voice was sharp, a feminine bark that echoed in the room.

Atlyn knew better than to react. Her heart was pounding in her chest. Did she know? How could she know that Atlyn had slept in Sayber's room? She'd been with her client last night on the main floor. Had someone seen Atlyn leaving Sayber's room?

The Mistress' body hit hers a moment later ramming the delicate tissue at her spine into the metal bar. There was a sharp pain, and then her legs went cold. *No.* Atlyn slid to the floor suddenly unable to hold herself up.

Myca gripped her by her throat lifting her as if she weighed nothing. Her fangs were at full length, her eyes like twin abysses in her face. Her nails dug into the delicate skin of Atlyn's neck releasing a thin stream of blood.

"You smell like sex! Who were you with?" Her voice cut like a razor. "Who!"

Atlyn couldn't answer, she couldn't pull in a breath past the vice at her throat. Myca jerked her farther up knocking her head hard against the stone wall. Atlyn saw stars but couldn't get passed the absolute terror of not being able to feel her legs.

The Mistress released her suddenly leaving her to

fall in a heap on the floor.

"Never mind. I'll deal with you later."

She turned as if she hadn't just damaged a person's spine, and waived her hand at the others.

"Begin."

Atlyn was left there as the others continued their class. When they practiced leaping each student had to leap over her as if she wasn't there. Each of them knew what it would mean to acknowledge what Myca had done.

Atlyn wanted to sob, but couldn't. Her legs were like ice, her brain felt like it had swollen too big for her skull. The class went on for two hours and she lay there in agony the entire time. What if she didn't heal? She healed slower than most because she wasn't allowed a full satiation.

Could she stand to live her life like this? Broken. Un-whole. Tears trickled down her cheeks and her chest heaved with each breath she took. Finally the class ended and the students left. To Atlyn's great relief Myca left the room as if she'd forgotten her promise.

The lights were turned off and the doors locked from the outside. Her Mistress hadn't forgotten at all. Atlyn was being punished. Treated as if she weren't even a person. Anyone who helped her would be severely reprimanded. Atlyn was afraid to move. What if she couldn't? What if the damage was to her entire body?

A cry burst from her lips, and she rolled to her back. Her legs were at an odd angle and she still couldn't move them, but at least she knew that her arms still worked. Pushing herself up she tried to drag her unresponsive legs to a more comfortable position.

Agony shot through them at her touch. She almost wished for the numbing cold to return. The pain was intense and she whimpered, laying back on the floor. Her eyes squeezed shut and she fought not to scream into the empty room.

She didn't know how long she lay on the hard wood floor of the dance room. The pain began to subside and she found that if she stayed very still it didn't return. She wanted to fall apart. Instead she held the image of Sayber in her mind. Wrapping herself in the memories of the night before. She would suffer anything to be near him. Even this.

CHAPTER FOUR

Sayber clicked the little icon at the top right of the screen and logged out of his laptop. It was the twenty first century but most Todesgeist still lived like it was medieval times. Humans were respected and treated as cousins to the race. That didn't mean that the Noble Kuspit intended to mimic their ways. Surfing the internet was a necessity, as was email, plumbing, and electricity, but it was a rare occasion that you'd find a television.

Sayber enjoyed a good romantic comedy, but he'd be damned if he'd tell anyone that. His mind wandered a moment as he imagined taking Atlyn to a movie. The thought brought a smile to his face. She was an innocent in more ways than one. She'd be amazed at what went on in the world outside the walls of a Noble house.

She was his mate. The knowledge was still new and enticing. He hadn't been looking for her. Hadn't thought that he'd find her so soon. He'd taken the appointment as Reticine to Myca on a whim. It gave him a chance to be independent from his overbearing father. Being raised by a Sangeisten had its advantages. It also had its disadvantages.

Now fifteen years later he wished he could have predicted what would happen. Myca had turned out to be a demanding charge. The idea that he'd fought for six hours straight to win the honor of caring for her was laughable now. If any one of those honorable idiots had known what he would be getting…He shook his head. They'd have all run the other way as fast as they could.

She'd seemed so sweet with her fair hair and eyes, and the slender curve of her body. Watching her dance had been like seeing the moon rise for the first time. She was practiced grace and fluid beauty on the stage. Unfortunately she was savage dominance and demandingly vicious in every other aspect.

Up until this point he couldn't say that he hated her. He'd just been ready to move on. But now? Knowing the way that bitch had terrorized his Atlyn, tortured her at every turn. Sayber rolled his shoulders forcing himself to relax his hands from the fists they'd formed.

He openly fantasized about wringing her skinny neck. He'd stood up to his duty, satiating her regularly, protecting her, meeting her every demand. But inside he seethed with the need to be away from her. It was like Myca was a plague and Atlyn was the cure. She was everything her Mistress was not. Sweet and innocent. Kind and thoughtful. And that little body of hers.

Sayber ran a hand over his spiky hair.

She was like honey on his tongue. He needed her like he needed blood in his veins. Just the thought of her filled his cock to bursting. But he couldn't have her. Reticine was an appointed position. Irrevocable. He couldn't quit. The only way for him to be released from the job was for Myca to find her mate and to formally release him.

She'd never do that. The evil bitch would never let him go, especially if she knew that he was Atlyn's mate. So in a nutshell....Sayber was screwed. Doomed to be a second to a female that he could hardly stand to look at.

Myca had that option. After finding her mate she could chose to keep him as her second. Sayber would then serve both of them. He shuddered at the thought. He wasn't into males. She'd tried to force one on him on more than one occasion. He'd refused flat out.

Myca was a sadist. He'd made the mistake of letting her know just how much the thought of it bothered him. She had made it her sole purpose to force him to do it. It wasn't that he had a problem with men loving men. He didn't. His oldest brother had mated another male.

Unlike the Demimorden love was love to his kind.

His father had welcomed his brother's mate with open arms and so had Sayber. Sayber just wasn't into it. The thought of being penetrated by another male held no appeal for him.

Of course that knowledge was what created his Mistress' ceaseless need to force just such a situation on him.

Sighing Sayber laced up his boots. His Mistress would be finished with her morning classes now. He needed to put in an appearance, or she'd come looking for him. It seemed petty, but since Atlyn had slept here he didn't want the witch anywhere near his bed.

He stepped into the hall and made his way to the training salon. Just as he arrived Myca stepped from the room. This was the second class of the day, the students in this group much younger and less experienced than Atlyn's class. The older apprentices trained in the other wing of the house. Sayber had to resist the urge to head that way. He needed to see his mate to make sure she was ok.

"Sayber." Myca's voice was low almost a growl.

"Mistress."

"Have you been a bad boy?"

He frowned. What was she talking about? "No." His voice was clipped, but he wasn't worried about hurting her feelings. She didn't have any.

"Are you sure?"

"Completely."

She smiled then as if life were a game and she the

31

game master. "Good. I had to punish one of the apprentices this morning for being bad." Her smile was delighted. "I know it's wrong but I love keeping them in line."

Her words hit Sayber in the chest like a metal beam. Who had she punished? His heart sped up. He had a feeling he knew who. "Do you need anything from me?" He fought to keep his voice even. Struggled to keep the rage inside him to a low simmer.

"Yes." Her hand cupped him and she sank her teeth into his pectoral.

He was completely unaffected, and glad of it.

"What? Not in the mood?"

"I am here to serve you in any way that you need." He grated the words, speaking against every desire in his body.

"I know." Her gaze shifted as she focused on something behind him. "Excuse me Sayber." She turned and walked past him. "Oh! Could you clean up the mess in the east training salon?" She said it as an afterthought as she strolled away. Not even bothering to turn as she spoke.

Sayber waited until she turned the corner and then turned in the opposite direction and ran flat out. His heart was in his throat. What had happened? It seemed like each step stretched into three more. When he finally reached the east wing he'd almost lost his mind to impatience.

Trying the handle to the training room he growled

in frustration when it wouldn't turn. She'd locked the door? Sayber hadn't thought to bring a key. He turned looking down the hall. No one was there. Gripping the door handle he wrenched it, snapping it at the base.

Great.

Taking a step back, he looked around the metal door. He could punch through it but he didn't want to take the time. He'd have to hit it more than once. Instead he kicked the broken handle until what was left hung loosely enough to pull off. Then he reached in with one finger and forced the trigger to release the wall.

The door swung open to reveal a crumpled body lying on the floor. The only light in the room came from the open doorway but Sayber knew exactly who was there.

"Atlyn." He whispered her name, then he was there crouching over her. Her eyes opened and it seemed to take a minute for her to focus.

"Sayber?" The wonder in her voice was a balm to his senses.

"Yes li'ya. I'm here."

"What? When?"

"Can you move?" He examined her body. Something was wrong. She didn't seem able to move. Her hands quivered at her hips, but her legs were leaden.

"My spine." She squeezed her eyes shut for a moment, and a single tear trickled across her temple.

"The Mistress she…hurt me. I can't move my legs."

Sayber saw red, his vision hazing behind the absolute rage that took his sanity. Only the small gasp from the slender body before him kept him from ripping the room to shreds.

"When did this happen." He cleared his throat trying to lighten the gravel from his tone.

"I was at morning training."

Morning training? She'd lain here for at least four hours! He wanted to scream his rage to the heavens. If Myca had walked into the room at this moment he'd have killed her on sight. His family's honor be damned.

"You haven't healed?"

"No. I don't feel any better than right after it happened."

Their kind could heal almost anything, but she was sène . The uninitiated were weaker, healing slower and needing more rest than a fully blooded adult. Still her body would be trying to right itself. The pain had to be almost unbearable. A slow burning agony. Sayber's teeth ground together. She needed to feed.

Sitting next to her head he lifted her carefully gasping with her at the movement. When she was resting against him he pressed his wrist to her lips.

"Feed from me little one."

She didn't hesitate, need overriding any reticence that lived inside her about feeding from the Mistress' keeper. Her bite was sweet and gentle. Pleasure dripped from her lips, filling his veins to bursting. His cock saluted her even through the pain and guilt that plagued him. His balls pulled taught beneath the shaft pulsing with the sudden need to orgasm.

Lusten filled the air around them and he was glad to feel her draw it into her body along with his blood. The change in her was almost immediate, her pain easing, her body relaxing against him. She moved her legs slightly and he lifted her off the ground cradling her against his chest.

He positioned her mouth against his throat and pressed a gentle hand to the back of her head. Her fangs sank into him and she drank deeply of his heart's blood. Nothing had ever felt better to him in his life. His cock jerked in his pants, the tip wetting with a warm jet of pre-come. He was close, needing her more than he'd imagined possible.

"Yes baby. Drink me in. Take what you need." He wrapped his mate in his arms, vowing that no harm would come to her again. Not if he had anything to say about it.

He waited until the pull at his necked lessened to a mere caress, then he stood holding her close to his heart. Without even thinking about it he took her to his room and laid her gently in his bed. She curled into the sheets moving much easier than before.

"Stay here li'ya." He pressed a gentle kiss to her forehead waited for her nod, and turned from the room.

He didn't think. He didn't hesitate. He strode down the hall each step making a satisfying thump against the mahogany floor. He reached his destination quickly and didn't knock before opening the door.

Myca looked up from her position on the floor. Her ass was in the air, her pussy being pummeled by the hulking male that kneeled behind her. They both looked at him, neither seeming to care about the interruption. The male's thrusts didn't even slow. He nodded at Sayber and continued to fuck his partner as if he wasn't there.

"You will never harm her again." Sayber's voice was ground steel.

"Who?" Myca arched her back raising herself into the thrusts of her partner.

Sayber was sickened by the haze of Lusten in the air. It was tainted somehow by the evil creature that created it.

"You know who."

"Oh. That little thing? She's hardly worth your time."

Sayber didn't bother to respond. He stared at her with dead eyes, wanting only to hear her agreement to his demand.

"Why do you care?"

"I care." That would have to be enough. He'd never tell the truth of what Atlyn was to him.

"What will you give me if I agree not to harm her again?"

He looked at her, disgust bubbling up his throat. "Name your price." *Bitch*.

The male stuttered behind her finishing in a forceful thrust, as he spilled his seed in her ready cunt.

"Yes, you can go dear." She smiled at him and sat back on her heals, her attention on Sayber. The male left the room, not bothering to dress before he stepped into the hall.

"I can't agree never to harm her. She provokes me by existing and I can't be held accountable for that." Her eyes found the ceiling as she seemed to think for a moment. "But I agree that today was a bit...harsh. It wouldn't do to damage her permanently. How would that make me look?"

Sayber remained silent.

"What will you give me if I agree never to do her permanent damage?"

If she so much as touched a hair on his mate's head he'd strangle her.

"What do you want?"

"I want you to submit to me."

His teeth ground hard enough to make his jaw ache. He had never agreed to be her submissive. Couldn't stand the thought of being at her mercy. There was no question of whether or not he would agree. Atlyn was more important to him than anything, anyone. That quickly, she'd become his whole world. His whole purpose for living.

"I will submit to you one time. If you agree not to

harm Atlyn again."

She made him wait several moments before responding. The snake in female form crouching on the shiny floor of her room, her pussy dripping with cum.

"I won't harm her again and you will submit to me tonight. And two other times that I choose."

Sayber nodded. He knew her word was as solid as smoke. She'd keep it only until she got what she wanted from him. He'd given her leverage over him by allowing her to see that he cared for Atlyn. She wouldn't let him forget it. He already regretted it. But it was the only choice he could make.

CHAPTER FIVE

She was alone in the world. Until this moment she had been completely alone. Waking up in Sayber's bed, feeling his heat around her, his arms holding her close, was the first time that she'd felt cared for in years. He was everything that she'd ever wanted in a male. Strong, protective, honorable. And more than that. When she was with him she felt as if nothing could go wrong.

That's what terrified her the most. The feeling of impending hardship was ever present. She'd felt this way every day since her father had passed away. It was a heavy weight to carry, a shadow impossible to shake. She wanted to fall into her mate, be drowned in him. But could she? She'd lost everything in life that mattered. What would happen if she lost him too?

Atlyn curled into the solid chest beneath her cheek. She refused to let fear keep her from reaching for what she wanted most. She needed Sayber to claim her before everything fell apart. And she was certain that it would. It always did.

She closed her eyes briefly at the tingling pain that still lurked up and down her spine. Today was an example. Had her Mistress meant to damage her back? It was more than likely that it had been a lucky accident. Of course she'd still enjoyed seeing Atlyn lying there in pain. Suffering each second as if it were a year of agony.

Atlyn rolled to her back, not bothering to wipe the tear that had escaped from the corner of her eye.

"Don't stew li'ya." The caress in his voice didn't lesson the scolding tone.

"I can't help it." She looked into his midnight eyes. "I could have lost everything today. If I can't dance…." She squeezed her eyes shut, taking a moment to push the unwelcome panic from her mind. "Why does she hate me so much?"

"I don't know." He ran a gentle hand down her cheek. "She won't ever hurt you like that again."

His tone was so final that Atlyn was afraid of what he'd had to do to be so sure. She turned into him, sliding an arm around his waist, and pressed her lips to his pectoral. "What did you do?"

Soft lips pressed her forehead. "Shhh. Don't worry li'ya. I will take care of you."

"And who will take care of you?"

Atlyn fought her shyness. She forced the ever present fear to the back of her mind. Quickly, before she could think about it, she sat up and pulled the light tunic over her head. She felt the cool touch of air on her swollen nipples, but refused to hide herself. Even though that is exactly what she wanted to do.

The look in Sayber's eyes was all she needed.

"You are beautiful. Did you know?"

"Will you claim me?" His smile made her bold. "I want you Sayber. I need you before we miss our chance."

She reached for him, pushing the shirt up the taught contours of his stomach, but getting caught at the shoulders. "Help me!"

He smiled easily pulling the shirt off, and wrapping her loosely in his arms. "I can't claim you." His hands slid to her hips, holding her in place. "Believe me, I want you. But I'm an appointed Reticine. I don't have the right to claim you." Regret brought a heavy tone to his voice.

"She won't let you go?"

"Knowing how much she hates you, do you think she'd let me go so that I can mate you?" As if unable to resist, Sayber leaned forward and flicked the erect tip of her nipple with his tongue.

Atlyn gasped, shocked at the wealth of feeling that came from such a small action. She palmed her breasts, enjoying the sensation of the rounded globes in her hands. She leaned into her male offering him her nipples.

He took her offer sucking the tips one at a time

into his warm wet mouth.

She moaned, loving the feel of his tongue and lips. "Please Sayber. Please take me. I need you." *I need to know that I'll never lose you.* She felt an urgency that was much more than sex. He was becoming her only anchor and she needed to cement that tie more than she needed anything else.

"Be patient baby. I'll make this right. I promise."

He lifted her laying her on her back and coming over her. The heat of him was a balm to her senses. But still she fought down a surge of fear. It wasn't that she didn't believe his promises. It was that she couldn't see how he'd be able to keep them.

He was appointed. In their world there was no way to become un-appointed. They took their roles seriously, so much so that breaking a vow like the one Sayber had taken could mean his life. The only way he would be free was if Myca released him. She could only do that when she found her own fated mate.

Sayber's hand brushed her cheek and Atlyn held it there with her own. Enjoyed the heat of his skin, the spicy smell of his arousal. Fell in love with him a little more.

"When did you know?"

He didn't pretend not to know what she meant. "When you first came you were still little more than a child. It took me a while to see you as more than that."

"A while? It's been seven years since I came of age!"

His smile was sweet and warm. She wanted to kiss it but was afraid to break the spell. His eyes caught hers and he leaned into her, pushing the hard evidence of his desire into her stomach. Then his lips where there pressing firmly against hers.

They were softer than she'd remembered, but still all male. He groaned low in his throat and she answered with a sigh of her own. Kissing her Sayber was heaven.

"I think on some level, I've always known you were mine."

"I knew you the first time I saw you."

"When was that?" He cupped her breast in one hand while running the other down the exact center of her body. He traced each curve and dip, his touch just light enough to stimulate.

"The day I moved to first apprentice."

He nodded. "I remember seeing you that day." He anchored a hand just above her left shoulder and she gripped his wrist, needing the connection between them. Her other hand itched to explore him. But she was still hesitant.

"Touch me li'ya." His voice was gravel, almost a growl. "I can't claim you, but I need you."

"I need you too, my Sayber"

She turned pressing a soft kiss to his wrist, then let her hands find him. He was firm and warm. His skin was soft. Leaning forward she traced his neck with her tongue. He shivered and she shivered in response.

His hands came around her waist and he pressed his hips to hers letting his erection nestle between her thighs. He still had loose pants on, but she could feel every detail through the thin fabric.

"How do you feel?"

"I feel better." There was still a little pain, but she'd never admit that to him. She'd been waiting her whole life for this.

He frowned at her. "Atlyn…"

"Shhh. You aren't getting out of this that easy. I want you. I think I've earned a little pleasure after today." She did her best impression of a haughty princess.

"You earned it ten times over."

He kissed her again, this time letting his tongue slip between her lips. Just a taste and then he pulled back to nibble at her plump bottom lip. She cupped his cheeks in both hands and brought his mouth back to hers. Tasting him as he had done, then dipping deeper inside. She felt her womb clench and her sheath was suddenly slick and ready.

Sayber pulled back. Breathing heavily he made his way down her body. "Open your legs for me."

She complied, spreading her legs as wide as she could with knees bent.

His eyes seemed to burn as he looked at her down there. She loved the way they seemed to glaze over with desire.

"Are you going to kiss my pussy?"

"Yes."

"Good."

He chuckled, then lowered his head between her knees. She felt his breath there first then the quick flick of his tongue. Atlyn gasped at the sudden spike of pleasure, then moaned when he kissed her slit with lips and gentle suction.

"Do you like that li'ya?"

"Yes." Her chest was heaving. She could barely hold her hips still.

"Let me know it."

He kissed her again, slowing at the end to lick her slick, swollen pussy lips.

"Yes. Sayber!" She moaned thrusting her hips into his mouth.

"That's it. Show me how much you like my mouth on you."

She sighed, letting her knees fall wide. She'd been forced to watch him pleasure Myca on many occasions. The pain of that. The torture of watching another female receive what had been created for her. She closed her eyes, unable to stop the gentle thrusts into his mouth.

This was nothing like she'd thought it would be. He suckled just hard enough to bring her back from the bed. Atlyn gripped the soft sheets in her hands, unable to stop herself from arching.

"Sayber!" She felt her pussy clench, a gentle flow

of wetness releasing from inside her. She was wound to the quick, like she could spin out of control at any moment. Sayber gripped her harder as if he knew exactly what he was doing to her.

"Give it to me baby. Let it go." His voice was a sexy rumble against her thigh.

His hands held her hips, locking her against him, and his mouth wrung every ounce of pleasure from her that it could. He'd started a steady suction, his fingers sliding thickly into her over and over. It was the perfect cadence. Sultry. Irresistible.

Pleasure hit her in a wave so intense that it was almost painful. Her body clenched from head to toe and her hips seized. Atlyn screamed, the sound breaking on a sigh as her pussy wept its enjoyment. Her womb clenched again, released, then tightened again, and again. Each contraction of her insides carried another wave of agonized delight.

"That's it. Mmmmm. You taste so good li'ya."

She shivered, as he blew a cool stream of air over her inflamed center. She was speechless. Her chest heaved and she couldn't seem to catch her breath. Atlyn managed to lean up after a while to look at the male that had given her the greatest pleasure of her life.

"Thank you."

His smile was a bright flash. "You're welcome little one." Leaning close he gave her one last lick. "It was my pleasure."

He took his time standing from the bed and carefully pulling the loose pants over his straining erection. His cock was turgid, large and proud. Her mouth watered just looking at it. She remembered the silken feel of his skin there. If she'd had the energy she'd have reached for him. Instead she settled for staring at him with hungry eyes.

"I want you inside me."

"I want to be inside you very much." He closed his eyes and reached down, his nostrils flaring as he palmed his cock gripping the heavy shaft at the base. An arc of *Lusten* filled with his potent scent flowed over her and she took him into her.

She'd been so overwrought with the feeling of him finally tasting her that she hadn't even thought to feed. His energy was spicy and rich and she was invigorated by it.

"Take from me li'ya. All that you can. You need to be satiated fully. You'll never be at full strength if you aren't."

"Will you break my sène Sayber?" Her voice was quiet, and he stood immobile as if he hadn't heard her.

"There is nothing that I would like more." He pumped himself twice, making long strokes from tip to base each time. The veins bulged in his forearm and he gripped himself hard. "I have no right to claim you while my life is promised in service to another. I won't shame you that way. Can you wait for me?"

She understood honor. Understood that he was

unable to take her into his life. She still couldn't prevent the small twinge of hurt that he'd rejected her offer. Her eyes followed his hand as it worked the thick shaft of his cock. She'd do anything to feel the hard length of him pressing inside her. The head of him was flared, a mushroom shaped pleasure nob built especially for her.

"Yes." Atlyn reached a hand out to him just grazing the smooth tip of him. His eyes opened suddenly. They were bright, burning with an intensity that she'd never seen in him. He stepped to the bed and climbed over her, caging her between his muscled forearms. His hips rested against hers and his huge erection pressed into her lower hip.

Sayber hooked one arm under her knee lifting her leg almost to her shoulder, while the other pushed her other leg to the side.

"I like you open and wet for me." He smiled as he kissed her sensitive lips.

She chuckled. "So do I. It seems like I'm always wet for you."

"Yes. A female's body always readies itself for a fated mate. Is that how you knew you were mine?"

"Yes. The first time... I felt pulled to you suddenly. It was the first time I'd ever been fully aroused. I went back to my room and rubbed my pussy until it was sore." Atlyn looked at his face to see what he thought of her words. Boldness was not one of her traits, but she felt bold with him. Safe as she'd never been with any other.

"Did you?" His voice was full of masculine pleasure, but also intrigue. "Do you rub your pussy often?" He whispered the last against the delicate cup of her ear.

Atlyn gave a soft shudder, enjoying the sensation. "Yes. Every time I see you my cleft feels so very empty." She closed her eyes as his lips tasted the skin just below her shoulder. His hips pressed into her and he slid an arm under her head. His eyes looked intensely into hers. He was very close. If she breathed deeply her lips would brush his.

"I want you Atlyn." The statement was stark. His body surrounded hers completely, his scent a spicy essence in the air. She was entranced by him. His mouth joined hers, tongue sliding inside, tasting. His hips thrust against her, nestling his cock against the slick wetness of her pussy lips.

He bathed himself in her, sliding the full length of his staff up, then down, so that he was coated in her flavor.

"Beg me to fuck you." He growled and his fangs dropped, extending fully. "Tell me to fuck your pussy."

His hips pumped into hers, the tip of him nudging her swollen clit. "Say it Atlyn." He pressed harder against her, faster.

"Fuck my pussy." She gasped. The head of him probed her entrance, pushing the nob of him into her small opening. He was just shy of entering her. One good thrust would have him sliding thickly inside her.

"Fuck my pussy Sayber!"

She wanted him so much that she felt crazed with it. Her legs wrapped around his hips, and she struggled against his hold. Her hips worked trying to force him inside her. Her movements pressed her against him more firmly, massaging her slit with the swollen tip of his cock. Atlyn loved the feel of him there. It was the most intimate massage she'd ever experienced.

Sayber remained still, not thrusting, just allowing her to move against him, the mouth of her pussy kissing the most sensitive part of him. Her hands gripped his shoulders, and she fought not to cut him with her nails. She felt frenzied, and was shocked to realize that she was close to release.

"Yes! Yes li'ya." He began to thrust his hips again, this time more slowly than before. He slid past her opening, rubbing himself against her soaked pussy. With each forward press he stretched at her opening bringing a ring of enjoyment through her womb, only to shift just before pressing inside.

He moved closer pressing his face into her neck as he gripped her breast with one hand. His palm pressed against her nipple, as his fangs grazed the pulse at her throat.

His hips fucked against her one, two, three more times before he groaned low and ragged. His fangs sank into her neck, and Atlyn added her own pleasure sounds to his. His cock released several hot jets of cum onto her stomach. His mouth sucked at her skin taking her blood into him.

The orgasm hit Atlyn sudden and hard. Her hips jacked over and over as she rode the tsunami of sensation it caused. His bite was heaven. She had never felt anything like it.

It was a long time before her body finally settled. Sayber rested against her a moment before sliding to the side.

"Thank you." His voice was hoarse.

Atlyn was still smiling when sleep took her a moment later.

CHAPTER SIX

"Assume the position slave." She let out a rough chuckle.

Sayber fought the urge to squeeze his eyes shut. Struggled with himself a few moments before he was able to make his knees bend to the floor.

"You know the rules. You don't speak unless I tell you to. My every wish is your command."

A shallow nod was all that he could muster.

"You may choose a safe word, but you may only use it once. After that you will have no reprieve from whatever I choose to do to you."

"Atlyn."

Her eyes narrowed, the mask of indifference slipping a moment at his choice. He'd chosen it as a symbol, a reminder to Myca that this wasn't for her. Wasn't about her, would never be about her. He didn't care how she took it. His true mate's face would be what would get him through this night.

The Mistress didn't respond. She turned, shedding the thin robe that covered her naked form. There were three males sitting side by side on a low bench against the far wall. All were as hard as pikes and almost as long. The *Ankhen* rode them. Their pupils were almost red in the soft light.

It was a drug often used on the uninitiated to prepare them for their first satiation. It heightened arousal, sensitivity, and increased the production of *Lusten*. It also aided in the opening of the *weile*, the place where the energy of the soul was produced. *Farbo* was the hardest of the three life forces to release and the most important. Only a full satiation could bring it out.

It was possible for a Todesgeist to survive on *Lusten* and *San* alone. But like his fated mate, they would be a weaker version of themselves. Slow to heal, and easy to harm. His Atlyn was *sène* , but wouldn't be much longer if Sayber had anything to say about it.

Myca walked in front of them, lips puckered, brow furrowed.

"My pussy needs attention! Who wants to show our Reticine how the Mistress likes to be treated?"

None of the males made a response but their already swollen, hard, cocks bobbed in reaction.

"First secure the slave."

Not needing any further instruction the three males stood and made their way to where Sayber kneeled. One moved behind him while the other two each gripped one of his arms. He felt the cold touch of steel as the shackles were clamped around his ankles and wrists. The three then stood and moved back to the bench.

"There that's better." Myca sighed lightly. "You get on your knees." One male did as requested, moving to all fours. He was large enough that his hips reached almost to the Mistress's waist. "Now you, my favorite, you may use him as a seat."

Sayber recognized the huge male from before. He was again naked and completely uncaring of his audience. He sat on the smaller male's back and spread his legs. His phallus was as large as he was and already moist at the tip.

Myca moved towards him slowly as if she were stalking her prey. When her hips were nestled between his knees she gripped his short brown hair in one hand and guided his mouth to her breast. He suckled her, his mouth making the wet sounds as it moved around the puckered pink nipple.

The Mistress let her head fall back moaning her approval of his handiwork. This went on for some time, before she removed herself from the wet clasp of his mouth. He didn't protest, didn't move at all until she offered him the other nipple. Then he began the process again.

Her sighs came more frequently this time until she'd had enough, stepping away from the male and turning her back to him.

"You may fuck my pussy Tebo, but do not cum."

The male grinned fully as he gripped the gentle swell of Myca's hips. Lifting her swiftly he was impaling her on his mammoth cock in moments. It was a stretch, and both groaned as he forced the girth of his shaft deep into her pussy. Then the Mistress was jogging up and down, taking him all the way to the root before lifting to the very tip.

She ground herself on him, working her hips in a circular motion as she cupped her breasts arching her back. Tebo, held her to him, doing most of the work, as he rammed his cock into her slit over and over. The muscles in his arms bulged with each violent thrust.

Myca grunted and moaned, her thrusts becoming irregular as if she were losing control. She came loud and forcefully, *Lusten* coating the air in spice. Sayber remained on the floor, the shackles a cool reminder of his subservience.

The Mistress stood as soon as her pleasure ended, the long manroot sliding from her dripping cunt with ease. She walked to Sayber, stopping when her mound was pressed against his face.

"Do you want to fuck me Sayber?"

He didn't answer.

"You may speak."

"No."

She stepped back from him, surprise a quick flash across her face. It was the first time he'd ever denied her anything. It was also the first time she'd ever asked him what he wanted. Myca saw the world as her potential slaves, taking what she wanted, without considering anyone else.

"I don't like liars Sayber. What do we do to liars Tebo? You may speak."

"We punish them mistress." His voice was soft but held the underlying force of a male in his prime.

She turned moving to the wall on the right side of the room. There was a metallic flash as she lifted something from a low shelf. Myca gripped the leather wrapped shaft of a flogger in her hands as she returned.

Sayber wasn't shocked at what he saw. The tool had long ropes of leather that were tipped with razor sharp spikes on one end, and a barbed ball on the other. Either side was perfect for ripping into skin and flesh. He'd seen what was on that wall in perfect light. This wasn't the worst thing that she could have chosen.

"Turn around slave and sit on your heals."

Sayber took his time obeying, crawling around, and dragging the heavy shackles as he positioned himself on his knees.

She sighed, then took a step closer, positioning herself perfectly for the first strike. She waited a moment, her breathing coming faster with each moment. The scent of *Lusten* in the air was thick with a slightly metallic aftertaste.

Sayber could smell the mistress' arousal. She loved

the thought of tearing into his skin.

"Tebo come here." Her voice was a soft purr from just over Sayber's shoulder. The big man lumbered to his feet and came to stand beside his mistress. "Our Reticine is reluctant to play with us tonight. I want to make sure that he gives us his full cooperation. Grip is cock in your hand Tebo. If he moves even an inch I want you to rip it off."

Sayber waited silently as Tebo kneeled in front of him finally settling into a crouch. He looked the male in the eye as the huge hand slid beneath his flaccid cock nudging his balls aside. Tebo's eyes were glazed but he looked very alert despite the drugs running through him.

"Do you have him in hand slave?"

Tebo nodded, his whiskey eyes never leaving Sayber's.

The first strike fell without warning. There was the ice cold sting of metal then the hot burn of ripping flesh. The copper tang of *San* filled his nose. Sayber felt blood well from the wound and run down his back. He did not make a sound.

The mistress continued, swinging the flogger with all of her strength. She didn't leave even a small square of skin unmarked. There was a puddle of blood seeping between Sayber's knees before she stopped.

The entire time Tebo had stayed motionless, Sayber's cock held gently in his hand. Sayber looked at the male taking in the highly aroused state of his body.

Tebo's penis made a gentle arch towards his stomach as it bobbed high in the air. His fangs were extended and his eyes glowed with a feral light.

The mistress took a moment to catch her breath. Sayber could feel her eyes boring into his back. She did not seem pleased with him. Sayber wanted to smile at the thought.

"Release him." The hand gripping him slid away, but Tebo remained where he was. Myca walked the few steps to Sayber and stepped over his ankle so that she stood just inches from his back.

"Did you like that my Reticine?" Her voice was a purr at his right ear. She gripped his shoulders pushing her thumbs into the wounds there as she spoke. A gentle intake of breath was all she received. Leaning closer she pushed erect nipples and high firm breasts into the bloody mess that was Sayber's back.

She gave a throaty moan, *Lusten* spiking the air. She rubbed herself in his pain coating her skin in the damage that she'd caused. Sayber gritted his teeth at the feeling of her tongue probing the wounds.

Her touch was agony to over sensitized skin. Her hands slid down to claw his buttocks and she rocked against him. "Do you like that Sayber?"

He didn't respond.

Myca released him and stepped back, her breath coming quickly. "Is he hard Tebo?" There was a slight lisp to her speech suggesting that her fangs were fully extended.

The male shook his head in response. There was the light tinkle of glass against glass, and then cool wetness spread over Sayber's bloody back. It mixed in with his blood that ran in a steady flow from the ruin that used to be his skin.

There were a few moments of calm as the liquid made its way down his spine. Then hell split the floor beneath him and swallowed him whole.

CHAPTER SEVEN

His fangs extended fully cutting through his bottom lip as his back curved into a tormented arc. He wheezed falling to the side as spasms worked their way through every muscle in his body. The world shrank to a pinpoint of space between one breath and the next.

It felt like hours had passed before his body allowed him to stop writhing on the floor. His eyes fell open and refused to close again. Myca lay on the ground next to him. The skin of her back slid in a puddle of his blood as she was fucked vigorously by the third male from the bench.

Her eyes were on Sayber as she gasped and grunted, her hips working her pussy into each punishing thrust of the male above her.

"I enjoyed that so much Sayber." Her smile was sweet in the dim light of the room. "Enough." The male stopped immediately, sliding the slick length of his dick from her pussy as he stood. He moved lithely back to the bench and sat down.

"Now for the good part."

The sound of her voice was wrong somehow, twisted beneath the sweet saccharine tone. Sayber rolled over, wincing inwardly at the sharp pull of pain at his back. He was painfully erect, swollen and pulsing with lust. His eyes felt unfocussed but his vision was clear. The fact that she'd drugged him was obvious.

He recognized the needy pulse of the *Ankhen* in his veins. It took the edge off of his pain, but the need he felt was almost overwhelming. He wanted the thick wet slide of his cock into his Atlyn's pussy with an intensity that was all consuming.

"Secure his hands Tebo."

The big male lifted the short chain of Sayber's shackles and clipped them into a thick metal ring that was bolted to the ground. Sayber was forced to lean forward far enough to put his elbows on the floor. His feet were similarly secured so that he had no choice but to stretch out on knees and forearms.

A clawed hand gripped the firm muscles of his right ass cheek. It squeezed, the nails digging into blood stained skin.

"You know what I want Sayber. Speak."

"You want what you can't have Mistress." His voice was low and rough around the edges.

"Who says that I can't have everything that I want?" She ran a finger up the crease of his rear. "Tebo is going to fuck you Sayber and you are going to lie here and let him. Do you know why? Speak."

"Why?"

"Because if you don't I will make your little apprentice wish she had never been pushed from the bitch that spawned her."

"Are you a liar now? You made a promise. I expect you to keep it."

Myca growled like an animal and struck, fangs sinking into the torn skin of his shoulder, ripping into the flesh. Sayber felt his blood gush from the wound and ground his teeth against the need to scream. The pain was more than enough to override any pleasure that the bite might bring.

She savaged him, shaking him like a tiger ripping into the hind quarters of its prey.

"Tebo! Fuck him until he cries for mercy." She spat and moved in front of Sayber as she wiped the blood from her mouth.

The Tellrian male moved quickly sensing his Mistress' urgency. He came behind Sayber, crossing in front of his face before sliding between his bent knees.

Tebo's cock was just as hard as it had been when they'd begun. His Farbo marks screamed his status as Tellrian Band, pulsed in a mildly metallic excitement on his hands and arms.

This one was as much of a sadist as his mistress. Sayber struggled to relax as the large hands came to rest on his hips. He felt the press of a wet cockhead at the puckered entrance to his ass and gripped his hands into fists.

There was a gentle steady pressure and he grunted at the slight burn as clenched muscles began to be forced to open.

"Tell him what you're going to do Tebo."

"I'm gonna fuck you until you beg."

Tebo groaned in anticipation as the heavy hips curved back in preparation for the first powerful thrust into Sayber's unready channel. *Lusten* poured from him, mixing with the copper sweetness of *San* that already filled the air.

"Atlyn."

The sound of glass hitting the wall punctuated the scream of rage that filled the room.

Sayber waited quietly for the male behind him to get control of his lust, and slowly step away. It was good that he had such restraint. Sayber would hate to have to kill him later.

There was a slash of renewed pain across his back even stronger than the first. Myca was in rare form even for her. Her fangs were long and sharp at the corners of her mouth. Her eyes were two pools of darkness in her face. The metal barbed lash made a faint whistling sound as she swung it.

One. Two. Three times. Each hit harder than the next. Sayber couldn't hold in a grunt after the third. He felt a slight shift in his chest when the barb hit. Felt like a broken rib.

"You were a *fool* to use your safe word so soon.

Now you have nothing to save you from me! You should have let him fuck you. Now I'm going to make you wish you had." Her voice was quiet. Each word perpetuated by the sound of the lash hitting Sayber's flesh.

Each strike brought with it a wave of agony so intense that wetness formed in Sayber's eyes. A scream welled in his throat and he swallowed against it, willing it to subside. She wouldn't break him. No matter how much she damaged his body. He refused to let her break him.

He held the image of his fated mate in his mind. The precious memory of her was the only thing keeping him focused. She was such a contrast to Myca. Gentle where the Mistress was violent. Compassionate. Sweet. She was everything that he'd needed in his life.

Nothing would keep him from claiming her.

CHAPTER EIGHT

There was only a whisper of sound as the door to her room opened, but it was enough to wake Atlyn from a deep sleep. The lights were blinding and then her wrist was shackled in the hard grasp of a male she didn't recognize.

"What…"

"Shut up." Myca was a nightmare. Blood on her hands and face, her pupils dilated so that they looked like pools of tar. "Get her up. Leave her clothes here." She turned and walked out of the door.

"Sayber?"

The male shook his head. His silence much more terrifying than if he had spoken.

"What happened? Is he ok?" The words were torn from her. She tried to suppress her terror. Failed. "Please…"

"It would be better for him and for you if you choose to cooperate." Lifting her easily he ripped the long shirt from her leaving only the cotton panties.

Atlyn covered her breasts with her arms her skin flushing with goosebumps.

"Be silent little one." He sat her on her feet but did not relinquish his hold on her wrist. She was pulled from the room and down the hall where the Mistress waited.

"Hurry up Tebo. He's waiting."

The male complied dragging Atlyn along with him.

"You'll regret the day you decided to come here. If you don't already." She chuckled, pausing as they turned a corner. "Sayber seems to be abnormally concerned with you. Don't get me wrong he's always been too soft hearted," she smirked at Atlyn. "He thinks that no one knows that he sneaks to the human theaters to see romantic comedies."

"Where is he?" Myca's gaze was sharp enough to cut. Her tone had been conversational, but she'd had no intention of talking with Atlyn.

"Don't worry about him. He is my business. After this, his little infatuation with you will end, and things can get back to normal."

Atlyn looked ahead of them shuddering at the sight of the blood read door at the end of the hall. What was Myca planning? She shivered deep in her bones. Where was Sayber?

"I told him that you would pretend to be afraid of him. That you would play the game he likes. You the scared virgin, him the big scary vampire. He was happy to break your sène . Excited that one such as you would be interested in playing his dark games."

Her smile was wide and mildly manic as she gripped the carved handle of the door.

"Do me a favor apprentice. Scream as much as you can."

Myca opened the door and shoved Atlyn in. She stumbled, tripping over the heavy rug that covered the floor. The room was dim, only a small lamp in the far corner giving off light. Atlyn shrank at the sight on the bed, backing into the door. The handle rattled as she tried to open it. *Locked.*

The male was huge, fangs completely extended, and his eyes glowed with an unnatural light. The air was thick with *Lusten*, and the faint after taste of fresh *San*. The bed was the biggest she'd ever seen.

"Come here little virgin." The male beckoned with one hand as the other gripped the base of a massive cock. It was swollen and heavily veined, straining towards his stomach in a gentle arc. His chest was peppered with markings declaring his status as a Kuspit.

Atlyn's heart pounded in her chest, and she knew he could hear it. Understood somehow that her fear was what he wanted.

"How is it that you are still sène ?"

She shook her head. Fighting not to imagine what he had in store for them. Her hands shook as she covered her face. A scream was welling in her throat.

He stroked himself, his eyes closing briefly, the muscles in his arms and chest flexing. Stepping from the bed, he made his way to her in mile long strides. Atlyn crumpled against the door, her knees bending into her chest.

"You are so sweet little girl. So innocent. I can smell it on you. You've never been fucked by a male have you?"

Atlyn squeezed her eyes shut. They popped back open at the sound of his hand roughly striking the door. He leaned over her his cock above her head, as he worked the shaft with his other hand. He licked his hand a few times, and continued to stroke himself, his eyes never leaving hers.

The room was filled with the sound of his hand working over wet, slick flesh.

"I can't wait to stretch that tight little pussy. Can't wait to be the first male to breach you." He groaned, picking up his pace, his hips thrusting into each stroke now.

Atlyn was shaking uncontrollably. Fear taking her voice, her ability to think. This male was going to *rape* her. Worse, he thought she had agreed to this, that they played a game. There was nothing that would convince him that this was against her will. She looked at him, taking in the heavily muscled torso and heavy thighs.

He was even bigger than Sayber. They were

opposites in color, this male had light hair, and skin that was so pale that it was pink. His eyes were like ice blue lights in his face. Atlyn would give anything to be looking up into eyes the color of midnight right now.

His stroke stuttered a moment and he growled. A hot jet of cum shot from his cockhead landing on Atlyn's nipple. He continued to stroke, milking his cock for every last drop. Three more releases gushed from him, coating Atlyn's breasts with his cream, before he was finished. It dripped over her nipples branding her with his essence.

She rested her hands at her sides, frozen in indecision. She wanted to wipe his spunk away, but was afraid that he'd react to her rejection. Would he harm her? Was he violent?

He stood upright releasing himself. A satisfied look crossed his face as his eyes roamed over her naked breasts.

"You look good covered in my cum. You'll look even better filled with it." He crouched in front of her, a hand cupping one drenched breast, then the other. He smeared his hand in his leavings, making sure not an inch of her chest was unmarked.

Making a feral sound he bent his head taking a nipple in his mouth, suckling hard. Atlyn gasped her hands gripping into fists. There was pain, and then strangely, pleasure at the feeling of his mouth attacking her delicate skin. He gave the other nipple the same treatment, his mouth making suckling sounds.

When he finished her nipples felt swollen and sore. Atlyn frowned, realizing that the sensation wasn't entirely unpleasant. It felt wrong underneath. This male was the wrong male. There was only one that she wanted to give her this type of attention.

He lifted her, his mouth pressing into hers. His lips were warm and wet, his tongue a marauding assault between her lips. She stiffened, whimpering in her throat as he kissed her. She pressed her palms to his chest, but was no match for his strength.

She landed on the bed with a light thump. He ripped her panties off with one hand while the other cupped her intimately.

"I wanted to kiss this pussy before I fucked it, but I just can't wait to be inside you. We have all night. I'll get around to everything I've fantasized about before you are initiated."

He gripped her thighs, spreading her legs wide. Atlyn froze, opening her mouth to speak. To say anything she could to stop him, but couldn't get a word past the knot in her throat.

The bed swayed with his weight as his knees landed between her legs. His cock was still hard, pulsing with lust. She could feel how much he wanted this. His own personal brand of ecstasy.

"Please…" A tear raced down her cheek. "Please don't do this." Her voice was hoarse, barely audible.

He shuddered at the sound of her voice, his shaft bouncing above her stomach. Cupping his sack in one hand he gripped himself pulling firmly while the other hand angled his erection toward her slit.

"Don't be afraid to scream if you need to." His voice was rough with desire. He spread her legs wider inching himself closer, the heat of him branding the sensitive skin of her legs and stomach.

CHAPTER NINE

"Sayber. For what it's worth. I'm sorry. I am…ashamed. The *Ankhen* is potent, more so if used often. I thought you were accepting of male attention. I would never have…"

Sayber blinked his eyes slowly coming back to consciousness. He hurt *everywhere*. There was a tug at his ankles and then the sound of metal hitting the wood floor. He sat up blinking in the dim light of the room. Tebo stood next to where he lay. A look of intense sorrow covered his square features. His eyes were clear now, the pupils completely back to normal.

"The Mistress will be very upset that I've released you. But after what I almost did, I couldn't stand the thought of what she's done to your female."

Sayber's eyes shot to the other male's. "My female?" His voice sounded like the turn of a rusty nail.

"The little apprentice? She is yours right? It is the

only explanation for what you were willing to endure. You don't enjoy the pain of the lash do you?"

Sayber shook his head, and almost winced at the heavy guilt that was added to the regret and sorrow that radiated from Tebo.

"Go to her now. She's been given to a patron. A kind of gift. Her sène , for his patronage. The red room."

The sound of metal rending shook the room as Tebo was thrown from his feet. Sayber didn't wait to see where the male landed.

His Atlyn needed him.

Sayber's mind was empty as he tore down the hall and up two flights of stairs. What if he didn't get there in time? He'd rip any male who touched her to pieces. His fangs descended nipping his bottom lip as he broke into a full out run. His tongue darted tasting his blood.

He hit the red door like a battering ram. The wood splintered under his fists dissolving before his eyes. There was a male hovering over his female, her legs spread wide on the bed. From one moment to the next there was the sound of a large body hitting the wall and then Atlyn was in his arms.

"Sayber?!"

"Are you harmed?" His voice was an unholy growl.

"No…I…He…" Her voice gave out.

Sayber turned toward the male, eyes zeroing in on

the still aroused penis.

"I'll kill you." He spat to get rid of the acrid taste of disgust.

"Sayber. Please. Take me out of here."

He turned back to her, clearly torn between his need to damage the Kuspit that had dared to touch what was his, and his need to care for her. He turned back gathering her gently in his arms and walked out of the room. He'd get her cloths and then they would leave this place.

Her room was closer but there were things he needed in his own. His door was open when he got there. There was a light on and a tray of food on his bed. *Tebo*. The male had turned out to be a male of worth. It was obvious that he felt a debt to Sayber.

"Sayber?"

He turned to his mate. He'd sat her on his bed intending to pack a few things and then leave.

"You are hurt?" her voice quavered and he cupped her cheek in his palm.

"I will survive. We are leaving this place. Let me get a shirt and shoes."

"No." Her voice was firm a stark contrast from the weariness of before. "No. If we go you will be called an oath breaker, Mor'do. They will hunt you and kill you. You must find a way to be released."

"I can only be released if Myca finds her mate, and even then only if she chooses to do so."

Her eyes were big in her face, wet on the surface.

"Then we stay until you find a way to make that happen."

"No. We can become Todesgeist, hide with them, pretend to a suburban couple. There are places we could go. Believe me."

"No. The warriors would find you. We'd never be safe. You must be patient. Please." She sagged forward, her hand resting against his bloody chest. "I feel sullied. Dirty. Like I'll never get clean. Can we take a shower?"

He couldn't deny her. Lifting her in his arms Sayber carried her to the bathroom. He didn't wait for the water to cool before he stepped in. Turning his back to the spray he winced at the sting of the water on his wounds. He checked her again for any damage. Her skin was smooth and unblemished.

"What did she do to you?" There was awe and anger in her voice.

"You noticed that huh?" He smiled and kissed her softly, careful not to press her bruised mouth with his fangs.

"Sayber, I should tell you…he didn't"

"Shhh. I don't care. You are here with me. I am here to take care of you. I promise you no one will ever be allowed to hurt you again."

"And what about you?"

"It's nothing baby. Nothing worse than anything else I have suffered at Myca's hands. It will heal. Will you?"

She nodded. Sure while looking into his steady eyes that she could withstand anything to be here with him. She looked down at the pink water that ran down the drain.

"Take from me Sayber." Atlyn tipped her chin baring her neck for him. "Please."

"Later."

He stepped from in front of the now warm spray of the shower. Reaching for the soap, he began lathering her chest focusing on her still red nipples and chest first. She wanted to sink into him. Sink into the feeling of his hands on her body.

"That feels good. Replace his touch with yours Sayber. Cleanse me with your body."

He hugged her to him his hands roaming her back and buttocks cleaning and caressing. He kneaded her backside, pressing her into his arms. Her breasts were a soft cushion against his chest.

"I want to touch you but I'm afraid I'll hurt you."

"You can touch me however, wherever you like." His voice was sinful, dark with promise.

That brought a smile and she slid gentle hands around his neck. Sayber paid special attention to every inch of her body. He stopped to massage and kiss each inch of her skin. His tongue darted out to taste her, as his hands soaped the trauma away.

Slowly as he claimed every part of her, his fangs began to recede. His arousal was growing by the minute but he had no intention of acting on it. She'd almost been *raped*. He wasn't going to add to that experience by trying to slake his lust on her.

Finally he finished turning her in the spray to wash the soap from her slick, lithe body. Her skin was glowing beneath the flow of water, her nipples offering themselves to his mouth. Sayber could smell her arousal.

"Let me wash you."

He was tempted, but thought better. He quickly washed the blood from his body and rinsed. Grabbing a towel from the shelf he wrapped her in warmth before reaching for another for himself. He carried her to the bed, and crawled in after her wrapping himself around her.

"We'll rest a minute. Then we have to leave." His eyes were suddenly heavy, his body turning to led limb by limb.

"Yes, my Sayber. Rest."

He fell asleep before he could answer.

CHAPTER TEN

"Sayber."

Sayber cracked an eye open, chagrined to realize that they'd slept the day away. Tebo stood next to the bed looking down at him and Atlyn. She was still asleep.

"The mistress is calling for you."

Sayber nodded. The mistress could get fucked. He and Atlyn were leaving here today.

"I think you should go to her." The look in his eyes was earnest, pleading even. "There is someone here. I called him. Reported..." He looked away as if embarrassed to admit it.

"You called the Sangeisten?"

"Yes. What she did is against the law. The Ritual demands that she cherish you, her trusted protector. She has not. Does not cherish. She violated you. I owed you as much."

Well damn.

As Sayber walked into the Mistress's show room, a large swollen glans was just forcing its way into the tight unready channel of her body. She keened low and guttural as it made its way in, the length of it stretching her pussy to new dimensions.

Relief washed over Sayber. It looked like his Mistress had found a new lover. It was his duty to care for her until she found her fated mate, which included the servicing of her body in the act of satiation. Not that he intended to perform any of his duties for her ever again.

He'd been an automaton going through the motions for almost fifteen years now. He'd lost his fervor for his appointment right around the time Atlyn had arrived.

"Mistress you called."

"Sayber!" Her eyes were glazed, blissful as she looked at him with new awareness shining in her expression. "I've found him."

Cocking his head to the side Sayber took in the man who was serving as a seat for his charge. He was well muscled and looked large, his Farbo markings declaring his status as Sangeisten and Tellrian Band.

They ran the length of his arms, and were only complemented by the family crest tattoos that made an elegant ring around the base of his neck. As customary for the Noble Protectors, Sayber imagined there was also a similar ring around the base of his cock.

This must be the male that Tebo had called. But

why was he fucking Myca?

"Sir Reticine," the male nodded in respect, "thank you for caring for my Myca all these years. I am happy to claim my mate, if you have no objections."

"Who are you?"

"Layte Santague, Sangeisten, and newly appointed chief in this area. Imagine my surprise when I arrived to find that the female that I'd come to question was my fated mate. And that she shares the same…proclivities as I do."

"Isn't he beautiful Sayber?" She kissed her mate open mouthed, as if she was unable to resist the allure of his body. "Don't worry my Reticine you will be my second, I won't cast you out."

Sayber's heart pounded in his chest. Second? Did she know about Atlyn? He wanted to scream his denial, and barely kept himself from shaking his head at her words. Did she not even think she had to consult him?

After all these years, he'd met her every need, and she didn't realize that he might have wants, needs of his own? He was bound, only she could release him. Ducking his head to hide his reaction he was silent, unwilling to congratulate her. Sayber refused to pretend any more. After what she'd tried to do to his mate he'd be happier if she were rotting in a gutter somewhere.

He felt eyes on him and looked up to see an expression that seemed like understanding pass over the Sangeisten's face.

"Do you object?" Layte said forcefully.

The words formed on Sayber's tongue but no sounds escaped. Object? He looked again at the man who was even now pumping steadily into his mate, and was caught in the compassion shining from light green eyes. It was as if he was trying to tell him something.

Had he been that obvious? As appointed Reticine he could not object to her choices, he'd fought for the right to be her honored protector, promised to put her needs above his own for the duration of his appointment, even if that was for the rest of his life.

The most he could do was to challenge her mate for his right to claim her. It was the ultimate disrespect, a step taken only when a fated mate was completely unsuitable for his charge. But Sayber had no desire to keep Myca, he was relieved that she would no longer be his responsibility. Why would Layte want him to challenge? Looking again he let his confusion show, shaking his head slightly and shrugging.

"If you have any problem with what your Mistress has said today, you do have the right of challenge."

He'd emphasized the last word. Sayber could challenge. And if he won he would remain Myca's Reticine, and her mate would have to leave his female unclaimed. If he lost…. Understanding bloomed in his chest. If he lost he would be cast from her life, his appointment severed immediately. He would be *free*.

But the dishonor, the disrespect he'd be paying this obviously honorable male? Could he take such a step against one such as him?

Images of Atlyn played through his mind. Her soft skin as she shimmied against him in the throes of climax, her hands slender and elegant as they gripped him, and the silk of her hair as it draped over his chest.

He was so close to his ultimate desire, could he do what was necessary to have her? His hands gripped into tight fists, his body bulging outwardly at his internal struggle.

Kneading Myca's bottom Layte sank his fangs into her neck bringing her to instant climax, then laying gentle lips to her brow he lifted her from his still swollen cock and lay her on the bed beside him. Bending slightly he pulled a short blade from his belongings and stood tall and proud before Sayber.

"Your Reticine wishes to challenge me for you my mate. Give us a moment to settle this matter." He tossed the blade to Sayber and reached again into his bag to pull out its twin.

Sayber caught the offered weapon and looked at Layte with new eyes. He'd just made Sayber's choice for him. Nodding slightly Sayber brought the knife to chest height and began the Ritual passes of the mate challenge.

CHAPTER ELEVEN

Atlyn's fangs extended at the sudden smell of pungent aromatic San. Turning she gasped at the sight of Sayber. He was bloodied, wounds still bleeding, and cloths torn.

"What happened?" She was breathless with worry, her hands curving into fists rather than complete the action that her heart desired.

"You are mine." His voice was a feral growl, his fangs fully extended, his eyes a burning beacon below his brow.

"Yes."

"Come."

Atlyn watched his ragged breaths as she made the few paces to reach him. Her hand fell over the already healing wound, and her face turned up to his.

"Please Sayber. What happened?"

She was pulled against him, a small sound escaping her throat and then his fangs were sinking into the skin where neck met her shoulder. The pleasure was instant, a burning wave of intricately wound sensations that shrilled over her body and inside in one sonorous note.

He brought her with his first pull on the wound and her knees gave, leaving her sagging into his bloodied chest. *Lusten* was a shimmering translucent sheet in the air, and she felt him draw on it, his chest expanding, as his throat worked to take in her blood.

"Yes."

"Need you. Sorry next time for you." He mumbled, and then her short tunic was ripped from her body. Her stretchy dance pants and panties followed immediately after. She felt the cool air of the room flow over puckered nipples before strong hands at her hips turned her to face the window.

Sayber lifted her knee, forcing her to place her foot on the window sill, and then bent her slightly at the waist. His body was a ferocious heat at her back, his breath coming in even puffs that blanketed her sensitive nape.

She shuddered as his hand found her wet and open for him, and then he was shoving himself deep into her body. The swollen head of him forced its way into her pussy stretching her untried muscles. With a powerful thrust he pushed it past her small opening, and braced a hand against her lower stomach as he heaved the shaft in after.

"So tight. So fucking tight."

Atlyn whimpered in pleasure-pain at the feeling of her mate finally entrenched in her body. She felt full deep inside, and fulfilled in a way she had never been before. The stretching of her channel was a mix of burning pleasure and slight discomfort, but she didn't care. They could stay like this, with him stretching inside her forever.

Sayber rocked his hips back slowly, letting his shaft caress her insides inch by sensual inch until just the head rested at the mouth of her slit. Then he thrust again, his fangs sinking into her upper shoulder, just as his erection sank in.

She made a sound much like a squeal as he pushed all the way in this time, not giving her the time to adjust to the length of him. He licked the wounds he'd made as he felt her convulse around him, the inner muscles squeezing and releasing in an orgasm.

Her cream was slick and warm around him, seeping from the lips of her pussy, as he pumped his cock into her over and over again. His hand traced the small waist and around to the sensitive underside of her breast. His palm found the tightly bound nipple and the tip as he cupped the weight of one then the other.

He was frenzied with his need of her his lips drawing lines over her neck and back as he braced her against him pushing her body with his hand to meet each of his swift entrances.

His pace increased, and she began a keening moan

that went on and on, climaxing with each piston of his hips at her backside. Sayber gloried in the softness of her butt cheeks as they cushioned his thrusting hip bones. She was his! He couldn't believe it, he was free, and this beautiful female was his!

He broke mid thrust, his orgasm coming over him in a gut twisting wave of such intense feeling that he bent them both over the sill in its intensity. His body shook, muscles quaking with each gush of his scalding hot seed into her body. A growling sigh escaped his pursed lips, and he hugged his mate against him until it was over.

Breathing profoundly Sayber lifted Atlyn in his arms, after gently disengaging his still erect penis from her body. His wound had almost closed, but he didn't notice as he looked down into the eyes of his mate.

"I'm free Li'ya. Myca has found her mate, and I am free."

Her eyes closed at the news, a pink tear appearing at the crease.

"How did this happen?" Her voice was a whisper, and he had to strain to hear it.

"How did I get her to release me?"

She nodded.

"Tebo. He called a friend of his with the Sangestien. Reported what Myca had been up to. The male that came turned out to be Myca's fated mate."

She rested her head against him, her arms finding their way around his neck.

"He is so much more than she deserves. An honorable male. He knew my story, and helped me to force Myca to let me go."

They reached his bed before she could respond. Laying her gently on the sheets, he stepped back to remove his damaged clothes, pushing the still open pants over slim hips and well-muscled thighs.

"I don't want to talk about them. Lay back and open your legs for me Li'ya."

Atlyn was in full agreement. All that mattered was that he was here with her now. And he'd never let her go. She did as he asked and he helped to position her just as he wanted, pushing her knees back until she was completely open to his gaze.

"I was too rough before, but now I'll make it up to you."

She moaned her response as his lips were suddenly against her wetness, his tongue making soothing strokes on over stimulated flesh. He suckled her clitoris and she couldn't stop her hips from jutting into his face.

Her body was a maelstrom of ecstasy, each teasing touch almost unbearable to her overwrought senses. The words of the mating ritual poured from her mouth before she even realized what she had said.

"This body is yours. This blood is yours. This heart is yours."

Sayber froze at her words, his mouth hovering over its target a moment before he reacted. His weight was a welcome balm against her and then he was fitting himself to her entrance again.

"This breath is yours. This strength is yours. This soul is yours." He responded, punctuating the last vow by pushing inside her, fitting into her perfectly as only he could.

He began a gentle shafting then as the ritual demanded. He would bring them to climax three times, both of them reciting the final three vows to each other at each one, before he could finish.

Sayber pulsed inside her as he lifted one of her legs over his shoulder to intensify the angle. He began to stroke long and steady, in and out, in and out without pause. His eyes held hers the entire time, the onyx-blue orbs ripe with promise and bleary eyed elation.

The first climax came on them as a gentle wave cresting and ebbing, each time with more force. Sayber took her mouth swallowing her cries, never slowing his pace.

"I trade my life for yours."

"I trade my life for yours." She repeated.

Rolling with her tucked tight against him, Sayber gripped her hips as he positioned them with her straddling his waist. He held her tightly just below the hip, not allowing her to move, as he fucked her needy pussy, ramming his swollen shaft up into her over and over.

Her back bent, breasts thrusting toward the

ceiling as she shrieked her pleasure for all to hear. Still Sayber continued, his pace quick and punishing. She leaned over him, sliding her tongue over his lips, and then dipping it into the sweetness of his mouth.

Her hips rocked with the intensity of his drives, her breasts swaying with each resounding pump. He caught her nipple in his mouth gently scoring the skin there, and Atlyn came in a back bending spasm of delight, her insides gripping him like a fist.

Sayber followed her shooting his man cream into her pussy filling her with his cum.

"I bind you with love everlasting."

"I bind you with love everlasting."

Their voices melded in the hot air around them, dancing through the *Lusten* infused room. Sayber brought her leg over his chest, turning her to the side, never once relinquishing his tight mooring within her. Helping her to lay in front of him he turned to his side, his hips spooning hers. His knee found its way between her legs, his other leg remaining strait.

Atlyn opened her thighs resting her ankle over the back of his knee, her eyes focused on where they were joined so perfectly. She felt a rush of elation with each plunge of his phallus into her snug channel. Never had she felt a sensation so dear, never had she imagined it could be like this with him. Her mate. He slid into her faster and deeper with each undulating rendition. She couldn't get enough of him inside her.

Sayber pushed his forearm against her lips silently

pleading with her to take his blood. She complied sliding sharp fangs into his skin and taking the life giving *San* from his vein. He did the same, biting her neck just below the first bite he had made, his hips continuing as if of their own volition. Her body jerked and she felt a profound tingle from deep inside her as if she were opening from within.

"Your weile. Let it come Li'ya. Relax against me, take me in all ways. "

His cock was a ram at her gates, splintering pleasure throughout her body with each inward plunge, tightening her insides into an achy ball just at the base of her stomach. She continued to watch as he took her, her wetness easing his way into her snug channel, and cupped her own breasts in her hands. She threw her hips back at him, meeting him push for push, never relinquishing her intimate clasp on him.

Atlyn's weile released abruptly pushing them both over the last precipice. It opened inside her liberating the essence of her soul, even as it fed from the essence of her mate's. With each never ending contraction and release of their bodies they drank of each other sating all three parts at once. Lusten, Farbo, San. They were one flesh, writhing in the agony of prolonged climax.

"I keep you with truth and faith." His voice was jagged, almost broken, as the final words were forced from his throat.

"I keep you with truth and faith."

Still they climaxed, over and over wringing moans

and growls from them both with each rolling assault. Sayber emptied himself into his mate's womb, but with each shimmying crest he found more of his essence to give.

Already his seed was gushing from her insides coating her thighs and his in their love. Her intimate embrace on him never relinquished, squeezing him with almost bruising force at each peak. Until finally the mating subsided, letting them fall boneless against each other, their breath sawing from their lungs.

Struggling against useless muscles Atlyn turned to face her mate repositioning him inside her even though he was already growing limp. She rested her head on the damp skin of his chest, her hand snaking its way to his shoulder. She examined her arms, marveling for a moment at the new *Farbo* markings that had appeared there. She was sène no longer! Contentment fell within her, filling her mind with uninterrupted peace.

"I'm yours," she said, and smiled.

"And I'm yours li'ya. Forever." His smile was just as bright as hers.

Turn the page for a
preview of Mercy's next
novel
in the Kingdom of
Nareth Series…

Lusten

Coming soon to
paperback, eBook and
kindle!

Only a fated mate could know her deepest needs......

The reinforced rod was cool and smooth against the skin of her inner thighs. Squeezing polished metal between her legs Destyni wrapped her ankle around, and let her body slide down the pole. Her hips pumped undulating her body in sensuous rhythm. She ran her hands over her flat stomach and up over well presented breasts before caressing the pole above her head. Her fingers grazed the marble floor of the stage only briefly before she flipped her legs down in an agile move that presented her rounded firm backside to the crowd.

Gripping her ankles she bent her knees, waving the soft mounds of her rear in a circular motion before standing upright again and cupping her lace covered breasts as if she meant to offer them to the male sitting in the first row. The music was upbeat, and pulsing, a complement to her dance in every way. Rocking her hips, Destyni shimmied her shoulders as she let the thin straps of the half halter slide down her arms.

Lusten was a haze that was almost tangible in its

abundance. The rapt audience gave it off in pulsing waves that matched the sway of her hips. Turning gracefully, Destyni let the half halter fall to the stage, and covered her nipples with her palms. She moved slowly, rolling her hips, working her body in simulation of hot passionate sex. The anticipation built to feverish frenzy.

There was an even mix of Todesgeist and Demimorden in the crowd this night, which accounted for the marked level of restraint her brethren were showing. On another night she would already have been pulled from the stage, by one of them, her neck and body pierced in one action. She wanted to sigh at the thought, but hid her sudden melancholy with a rolling turn that brought her mostly nude form back to face the crowded room. She was an appointed Feeder, at the LeiberSan, a mid-class Blood Dèn in southern California. Though the choice had been forced on her, she had long since accepted her fate.

She dropped her hands and felt the surging emotions like a tingling breeze against the sensitive skin of her breasts. Her nipples responded immediately becoming erect daggers at her chest. Looking out over the crowd she walked up the narrow outlet, moving in a way that caused her chest to bounce and jiggle in a supremely enticing way. She knew the effect she had saw it in the raging signatures of the Todesgueist, and the softer less distinct ones of the humans. It was like translucent electricity that sparked in a firework display around each male.

The sight of it both attracted and repulsed her at the same time. She was an adult now, strong in her gifts and confident in her duties, but there was still a part of her that remember the scared girl who'd had adulthood forced on her in excess. Smiling mysteriously against the turbulent memories that attempted to bloom in her mind, Destyni finished her dance. Floating to her knees she crawled to the edge of the outlet and sat on her heals, all the while working her curvaceous form in time to the music. Laying back she rested her head on the floor and curved her back into a perfect lotus, serving up her assets to precision. She paused waiting for the last strains of the song to fade before she stood and walked from the stage ignoring the raucous applause that followed.

As the curtains closed behind her the temptress fell from her shoulders like a silken veil. She did what was required, had honed her body and mind to perform day after day, but she took no joy in it. Grabbing the plush emerald robe from its perch she clothed herself and stepped through the inner door to the dim hallway. She needed to feed. There was a slight tremble in her fingers, and she curled them into fists. She was on duty this night, and needed to attend at least the first presenting, or she would be punished. Each night she and the other Denkin of the LeiberSan were presented to the patrons on the hour until all had acquired assignations.

Her Blood Mother could not be called fair by any means, but Jyn did at least give the allusion of participating in the Ritual. The Blood Dèn had been established early on in the Kingdom, providing an easy place for unattached Todesgueist to feed away from the eyes of the Demimorden. Each had an appointed Blood Mother, usually of the Noble Kuspit that held dominion of all that lived there. They'd since integrated themselves into human society allowing them to blend into the current culture with ease. The LeiberSan was an elegant strip club to most Demimorden. It brought in a healthy crowd on most nights of the week.

She felt a vibration in the pocket of her robe, and she remembered her cell phone was there. Palming the small flat device she lifted it out and examined the luminous face.

A shrill voice ruptured the calm of the night freezing her in mid motion. Looking in the direction it had come from Destyni was shocked to see a naked Demimorden running towards her as if she were being chased by an army of the undead. Looking past the human she saw a shock of blue hair. Tien. Her Blood Mother's lover was a common sight at the LeiberSan, but not usually in connection with terrified females. What was going on? These were the back halls of the Dèn, humans were not allowed here. Stepping into the female's path she caught her at the waist, feeling the press of a naked female form against her.

"Are you all right?"

"Please." The eyes were pleading, the hazel irises almost swallowed by the pupil.

"What happened?"

Destyni felt the cool press of a gloved hand before she looked up at Tien. He was smiling as usual, his face curving to kindness with practiced ease.

"Thanks love." His voice was gruff, deeper than usual. He pulled the shivering female from Destyni's grasp, fighting clinging human fingers.

"What?" A curt shake of his head stopped her question. She looked at the male in question, noting the dark red tendrils of his signature that hadn't been there a moment before. It was violence, rising off of him like steam in winter. Destyni knew better than to engage him when he was like this. She'd learned long ago of what this one was truly capable. She barely held in a shiver as his body came close to hers. Turning with the female now cradled in his arms, Tien walked away without another word.

A feeling of wrongness assaulted her and she shut her eyes against it, willing the bubbling guilt to the back of her mind. She saw herself as the human, cradled against a muscled chest, caught in the gravity of deep red eyes. Tien was we-fe, what human's called albino. The Todesgeist version of the condition was much less noticeable, the eyes a crimson, the skin fair but not pale, and the colorless hair. They often utilized human mechanisms to hide their condition, hair dye and contacts went a long way to feign a sense of normalcy. Tien seemed only to favor the dye.

Memories battered her, shuttling weakness to her knees and she pressed a hand to the wall to keep from crumbling to the ground. It had been Tien who had initiated her into the life of a Feeder. He'd broken her Sène, bringing her to adulthood by completing her first full Satiation. He had not been gentle. He'd drank her tears like they were the finest ale, and had enjoyed the painful union of his body within hers.

Shaking off the cold mist of fear and pain Destyni forced her body upright, and willed her legs into motion. She'd see what she could do for the female later if she could. She was already late for the first presenting, she didn't even want to imagine what would happen if she missed it entirely.

ABOUT THE AUTHOR

Mercedes Bleau is an author of Erotic Romance Fantasy and Paranormal. She spends her days writing stories in the attic of an old Victorian, and her nights dreaming of Alpha's from different worlds…. Look for her next story in the Kingdom of Nareth series, *Lusten* in 2016, and the second book in the Books of the MagKaen series, *Witch Betrayed* just after the new year.